WANTED
ROYAL
COOK

This book is based on a story that
Julia Donaldson's son Alastair made up
for his daughter Poppy.

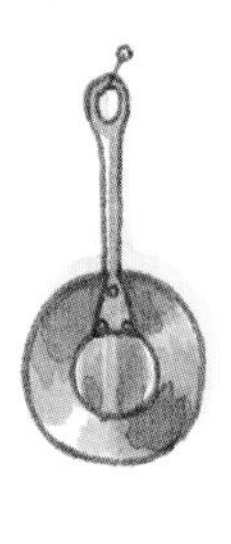

For Ally and Poppy
JD

For my nephew Joel, who only
eats crisps. From Uncle David
DR

First published 2018 by Macmillan Children's Books
an imprint of Pan Macmillan
20 New Wharf Road, London N1 9RR
Associated companies throughout the world
www.panmacmillan.com

ISBN: 978-1-5098-1377-3

1 3 5 7 9 8 6 4 2

A CIP catalogue record for this book is available from the British Library.

Printed in Spain.

The Cook and the King

Julia Donaldson David Roberts

MACMILLAN CHILDREN'S BOOKS

There once was a very hungry king
Who needed a cook like anything.

King
Pizzas

So he tried out lots and lots of cooks
With their pots and their pans and their cookery books.

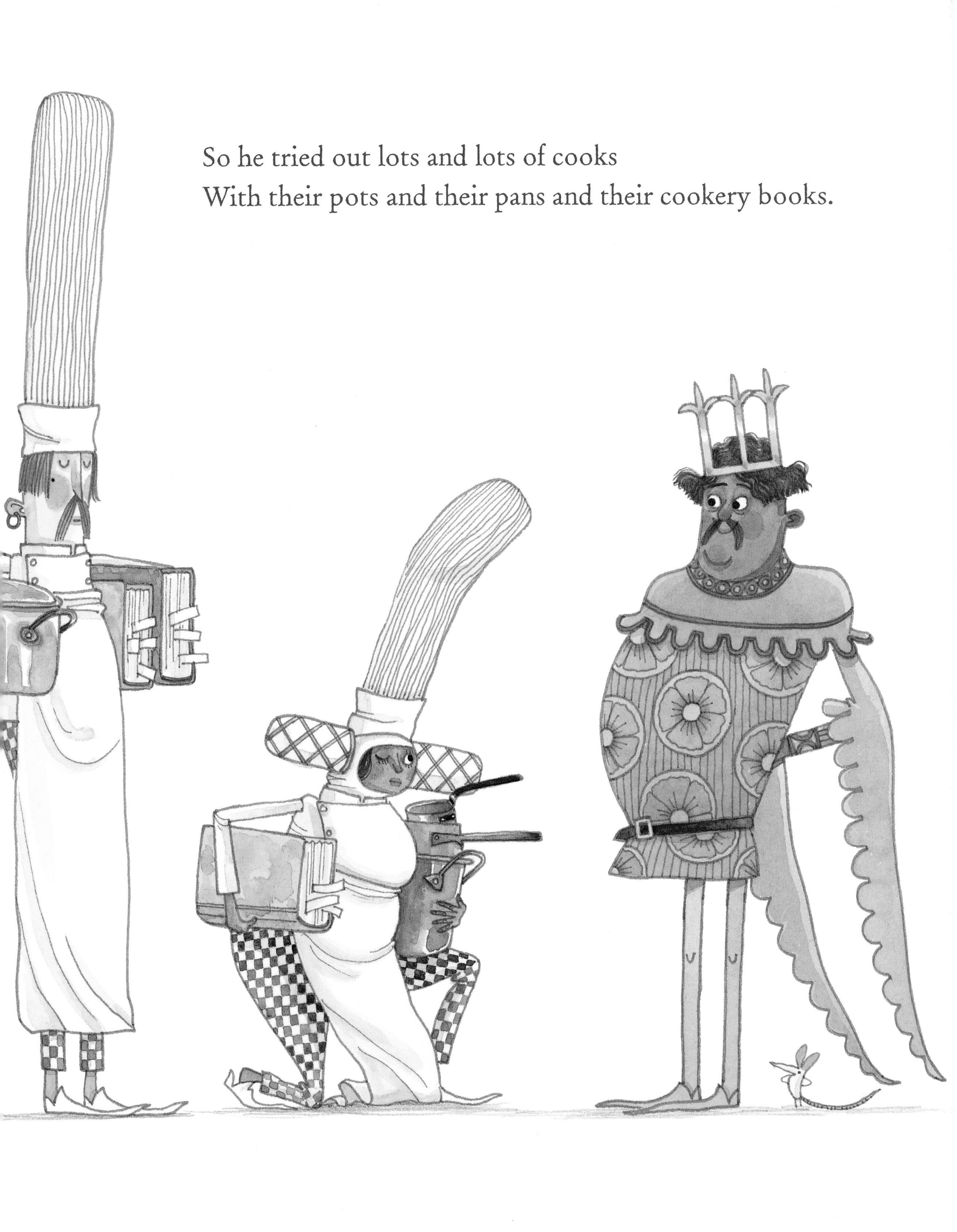

One by one they cooked for the king;
They cooked and they cooked like anything,
But nothing they cooked was good enough.
“This egg is runny. This meat is tough.

Too hot! Too cold! Too sour! Too smelly!
I don't want a sausage inside my jelly.
This tastes ALL WRONG," said the hungry king,
And he frowned and he frowned like anything.

But then he spotted another cook
With feet that shuffled and hands that shook.
"My name," said the cook, "is Wobbly Bob.
I'm a bit of a wimp, but I'd love the job."

The king thought hard, then he scratched his head.
"I fancy some fish and chips," he said.
"Yes, fish and chips is my favourite dish,
But first you will need to catch the fish."

"Help!" said the cook. "I'm feeling scared.
I'd love to fish if I only dared,
But a shark might land in the fishing net
Or I might get my nice new apron wet.
My knees are knocking," the cook declared.
"I'm scared! I'm scared! I'm terribly scared."

"I'll help you fish," said the hungry king,
So he fished and he fished like anything.
He caught some fish that were nice and big,

Then he said to the cook, “It’s time to dig.”

"Help!" said the cook. "I'm feeling scared.
I'd love to dig if I only dared,
But I'm scared of worms and I'm scared of ants.
They might crawl into my nice new pants.
My palms are sweating," the cook declared.
"I'm scared! I'm scared! I'm terribly scared."

"I'll help you dig," said the hungry king,
So he dug and he dug like anything.
Then he said to the cook, as he licked his lips,

"Chop these potatoes into chips."

"Help!" said the cook. "I'm feeling scared.
I'd love to chop if I only dared,
But knives are sharp and I might get hurt.
I might get blood on my nice new shirt.
My heart is thumping," the cook declared.
"I'm scared! I'm scared! I'm terribly scared."

"I'll help you chop," said the hungry king,
So he chopped and he chopped like anything.
Then he said to the cook, who was standing by,

"Out with the pan! It's time to fry."

"Help!" said the cook. "I'm feeling scared.
I'd love to fry if I only dared,
But oil can splutter and spit and splat.
A drop might land on my nice new hat.
My teeth are rattling," the cook declared.
"I'm scared! I'm scared! I'm terribly scared."

"I'll help you fry," said the hungry king,
So he fried and he fried like anything.

Then he set the table and took a seat
And he said to the cook, "It's time to eat."

“Good!” said the cook, so the two men shared.
“What great cooking!” the king declared.
“What well-chopped chips, and what well-fried fish!
All in all, a delicious dish!
It tastes JUST RIGHT,” said the full-up king,
And he smiled and he smiled like anything.

"Congratulations, Wobbly Bob.
You may be a wimp, but you've got the job!"

The End

WANTED
ROYAL